DATE DUE	4 / 01		
MAY 01 '01			
MAY 24 '01			
JUN 19 '01			
SEP 07 '01			
OCT 23 '01			
AUG 10 '02			
JUL 01 '03			
JUL 23 '03			
AUG 06 '03			
DEC 09 '04			
APR 05 '06			
AUG 31 '06			
GAYLORD			PRINTED IN U.S.A

Low Song

written by **Eve Merriam** and illustrated by **Pam Paparone**

Margaret K. McElderry Books

NEW YORK

LONDON

TORONTO

SYDNEY

SINGAPORE

Low Song

Margaret K. McElderry Books
An imprint of Simon & Schuster Children's Publishing Division
1230 Avenue of the Americas
New York, New York 10020

Book design by Ann Bobco.
The text of this book was set in Didot LH.
The illustrations were rendered in acrylic.
Printed in Hong Kong
10 9 8 7 6 5 4 3 2 1

Library of Congress Cataloging-in-Publication Data
Merriam, Eve, 1916-1992
Low song / by Eve Merriam; illustrated by Pam Paparone.   p.   cm.
Summary: Rhyming text celebrates various aspects of the world, from falling leaves and falling snow
to hushaby tunes and little new moons.
ISBN 0-689-82820-9
[1. Stories in rhyme.] I. Paparone, Pamela, ill. II. Title.   PZ8.3.M55187Lo   2001   [E]—dc21   99-20699

For Nikki
—P. P.

I like things that come nice and low
Falling leaves and falling snow

Puddles to jump

Sand to dump

Slidealong floors

Cellar doors

Somersault places
With upside-down
faces

Dachshunds' backs
Sidewalk cracks

Tires whizzing along the street
And the morning sound of the milkman's feet
Low low   go go
    Clop clop   stop stop

Pebbles

Shells

All flowery smells

Sloshing mops

Spinning tops

Barrels of pickles

Straw that tickles

Cowboy boots
Tree roots

Caterpillars creeping
Giraffes when they're sleeping

Sweet potato vines
Under-door valentines

A cow's tongue licking over
Pink and purple clover

Grass growing
Water flowing

Heels

Wheels

Flippery seals and slippery eels

Ladybugs

Plugs

Snuggly puppy hugs

Baby raccoons
Hushaby tunes
And little new moons

Good night!